A **Lillenas** DRAMA TOPICS SERIES

THEATRICAL MAKEUP

A Practical Approach for Church Drama

**by Ginger Shew
with illustrations by
Michael Shew**

**Lillenas** PUBLISHING COMPANY

KANSAS CITY, MO 64141

Some Personal Thoughts

It's 10:30 P.M. on a Saturday night, and you've put the last performance behind you. The group has dwindled to the regular members of "The Whine and Dine Café." You meet at the all-night truck stop or someone's house, gathered around cookies, sandwiches, and coffee.

You babble about things that went right, dream about things you hope to do better next time, and whine about things you'll never do again. Everyone listens, sympathizes, and pours you *another* cup of coffee.

Regulars at the "Whine and Dine":
Tim, Patty, and Ashley Freeman
Mark and Tammie Lowry
Mike Shew
Deborah Craig-Claar
Carl and Karis Moore
Thanks for endless support, and the "bottomless cup"!

Many thanks to:
Ron Boutwell, for your inspiring vision; to Paul Miller, for challenging me; and to my husband, for the extra push and help with the laundry.

Contents

Preface: The Play's the Thing 7

Chapter 1 9

    Health and Safety—Read This First!

    Why Do We Have to Use Makeup?

    Terms, Tools, and Gadgets

Chapter 2 13

    What's First?

    Hey! What's in the Tackle Box?

    Who Am I, and What Do I Look Like?

    The Basic Face (Everybody Has One)

Chapter 3 19

    Middle Age and Old Age

    Racial Makeup

    Plants, Animals, and Things That Go Bump in the Night

Chapter 4 25

    Hair and Wigs

    Beards and Mustaches

    Wounds, Bruises, and "Ouchies"

Chapter 5 33

    Making Up Children

    Creating a Makeup Notebook

    The Makeup Room—Enter with Attitude!

    Making It All Work

Appendix 37

    Leading Makeup Manufacturers

    Makeup Inventory

    Makeup Design Sheet

Preface

THE PLAY'S THE THING . . .

. . . that everyone has come to see. Makeup is a small but important part of being seen. Costume, props, gestures, and lighting also help the actor to become more visible onstage. I like to remind people that our eyes and ears work together when we receive information. It is surprising how much we communicate with facial expression and gestures in addition to our voices. You must see and hear to get the whole message.

So, with *being seen* and *communication* as our goals, I will "spotlight" on makeup and how it helps you achieve this. This book will focus on the needs and questions most beginners have, but I hope to give you enough information to get you through a variety of situations. Do not consider this the first and last word in makeup! That would only stunt your growth. Now, go find your face and a mirror; you'll need both for the rest of this book.

CHAPTER 1

HEALTH AND SAFETY—READ THIS FIRST!

People somehow get the idea that makeup is a hazard-free area, until they wake up with this awful rash. Please do not make this assumption. It will come back to "bite" you! There is a reason I'll tell you to practice with everything you try the first time; it may be the last time you try it! Some potential problem areas to consider in the makeup room are: allergic reactions, spread of disease, and injury.

Let's suppose you need to have white hair for a performance. You think all you need to do is spray this stuff on and go! Then the second time you put it on, your head itches a little because you really "didn't get it all washed out the night before." The next night is opening night and you just spray your head again, but you wash it out very well, and there's just a little redness because you scrubbed so hard. The next morning you notice tiny bumps around your hairline that you attribute to stress (and maybe that hair stuff), but you just have two more performances. By closing night you've already made a doctor's appointment for this raging rash all over your scalp, and you can't wait to hit the shower. You boldly pat yourself on the back, saying, "I am an *actor*, I have suffered for my *art*." (Not like you're going to suffer from here on, though.)

I didn't create this little story. My husband spent a year with a low-grade scalp infection that would heal in one area about the time it broke out somewhere else. The experience was most unpleasant!

I've heard a number of stories from other misguided folks thinking they "could handle the pain," they didn't want to bother washing their faces before going to bed, "trouble breathing" meant a cold coming on, or they just got a little of "that stuff" in their eyes. Until you have a reaction to something, you don't know you're allergic to it! When you find out the hard way, it can be dangerous! I can't tell you enough how important safety precautions are, but I intend to try.

If anything in this book implants in your brain, this should be it:

IF IT HURTS—STOP!

This seems a little simplistic, but I've noticed a lot of simple-minded people out there. **Don't ignore warning signs** such as: any swelling in the eyes or face, rashes, redness, or difficulty breathing. If any of this is occurring, **stop what you're doing.** There isn't a performance worth doing if it puts you at high risk. I hear you arguing with me, but if the three nights onstage cost you a week in bed or worse, something is very wrong. There are ways to work around problems.

There are some fundamental things you can do to help "save face," even if you have a communal makeup kit. Good general hygienic rules are:

1. **Always wash your face before putting on theatre makeup.** This keeps dirt, skin oil, and old makeup from imbedding into your pores, or transferring into your theatre base. (I always make sure my hands are clean too.)
2. **Before makeup, splash a little cool water on to help tighten pores.** It helps to keep makeup from imbedding in your skin.
3. **Keep your tools clean and dry,** be sure to carefully wash sponges and brushes in *cool*, soapy water. Wipe down and dry pancake bases before putting lids on and storing. Sometimes an overnight "airing" is necessary before putting the lids on.
4. **Wipe down items such as lipsticks and cream colors before the next person uses them.**
5. **Always wash your makeup off completely,** *never* sleep in it! Follow your wash with a mild astringent and a lotion suitable for your skin type.

6. **If you suspect that you have sensitive skin, a chronic skin condition, or a tendency for acne, you will be wise to invest in your own makeup. Don't share it! You will protect yourself and others.**

Sometimes, what appears to be an allergic reaction is simply a virus or bacteria that is growing on unclean items, or transferred from someone. For some people, the very process of washing, makeup, and washing again is enough to irritate skin that isn't used to it. Be gentle with your face, you've only got *one!*

To take the surprise out of allergic reactions, test everything first. You are probably already aware if you have sensitive skin. Don't ignore it for a performance. Test your makeup on the inside of your wrist; put it on and leave it for a few hours. Try the same test in the same place on the next day too. You may have no problems at first, but sometimes an allergy is "built up" over a period of time. For hair color, test it the same way. There are hypoallergenic makeups available, on request. If you have trouble with hair color, try having it professionally dyed or consider using wigs.

I think you can see the problems with allergy and disease; let's talk about potential physical injury. I know you can't imagine what you could do to hurt yourself. Let me help! The injury area covers all those little freak things that happen to more people than you might think. What comes to mind immediately as a hazard is *long fingernails.* I usually cut mine before working on anyone's face to keep from scratching them, or worse, poking out an eye! It's also easy to get makeup caked under your nails, and it's important to keep your hands as clean as possible.

Something else that gets people in trouble is the use of prostheses. (This means anything that is glued onto your face, put into your mouth, attached to your head, etc.) One danger here is getting glue off your face properly. **Do not use nail polish remover, turpentine, or ammonia-based products.** These will burn your skin! Use a cotton ball soaked in rubbing alcohol and carefully let the alcohol seep under the prosthesis. Then peel it off slowly. Use soap and water to remove the excess. *Be very careful around the eyes and the mouth!* I suggest using eyelash adhesive whenever possible around these delicate areas. **Do not** put things into your ears or nostrils; remember, your mother told you the same thing! Theatrical "false teeth" can be swallowed! Make sure you have practiced with them, and that they fit you well. Don't try eating with them in! Be careful with false noses, not just in the choice of glue you use, but enlarge the "nostrils" (if needed) to be sure you're getting enough air. Anything you fasten into the hair should be secure, but not *gouging* the scalp, such as fake ears, horns, hairpieces, and so on.

Other dangers to avoid include:

1. **Putting makeup substances in Styrofoam cups**—first, you're liable to drink it; second, there's a chance of spillage.
2. **Some items are *flammable*.** Spirit gum, nail polish remover, liquid latex, premade latex pieces, crepe hair, plastic garment bags, wigs, Styrofoam cups and wig stands are items indigenous to the costume/makeup room that will cause fires. Be careful with light bulbs, curling irons, and clothing irons. **Note: Burning Styrofoam and plastic are very toxic, and inhalation will cause brain damage.**
3. **Do not use *artist's paints* on your skin! They contain toxic materials!**
4. **Overcrowded makeup rooms can result in getting bumped while doing your face.** (Not something you want to have happen while lining your eyes.) Stagger your "makeup call" so that everyone has a little space, and encourage those that are finished to leave the area.
5. **If you have a rash or sunburn, see your doctor before you think about doing makeup.** You could start an infection!
6. **The obvious hazards:** leaving lights on, irons on, stuff on the floor, drink cups everywhere, and using electrical appliances while standing in a puddle of water. (Need I mention, "don't run with scissors"?) I usually wait till everyone is onstage, and then make a sweep of the backstage area. I fully believe that we should all pick up after ourselves, but . . .

There are a few other things to insure good health while getting through a performance. Sleep is always good if you can get it. Even a little extra nap before rehearsal helps a lot. A little extra vitamin C to take the edge off the "stress factor." *And most importantly* (my mother said so), *drink eight glasses of water each day!* Water helps keep your skin clear and lubricates the throat. If you're very active on-stage or doing a musical (more voice stress), drink even *more* water. It's one of the best things you can do for your body, period. Ask your doctor, or my mom. I also encourage you not to put yourself in risky situations before a performance: Mountain climbing, skiing, drag racing, crossing against the traffic light, and general horsing around.

In short, don't do anything to yourself that you'll be embarrassed to explain to the paramedics when they come for you.

WHY DO WE HAVE TO USE MAKEUP? (They Usually Whine . . .)

First, and most importantly—to be seen! There are a few factors effecting the visibility of an actor onstage. To begin with, you have distance between you and the audience: The further they are from you, the less they see of your facial expressions. Makeup enlarges your features, closing up some of the distance. This helps your audience read your expressions.

Lights! Intense light that makes everything onstage show up well will also shine right into your skin. Imagine laying several sheets of white tissue over a map. You hit it with a spotlight, and you can still read some of the map because it has all those dark lines on it. Your skin is several layers of thin, translucent material over blood vessels, muscles, and tissues. Without proper makeup, your blue veins will show up, giving you a very unappealing look under the lights. Most will look slightly blue or green, while others (myself included) will look like road maps!

Makeup helps create the character. I said *helps*. **The character comes from the actor, and makeup is only the finishing touch.** Once you know all about your character, the makeup is easy. Even if you are doing "straight" makeup, the psychological factor of "being finished" will give you a mental boost. If one is doing "character makeup" (i.e., not your usual face), the *look* will enhance what the actor *feels*.

TERMS, TOOLS, AND GADGETS

BASE: The first makeup used on the face. The base coat is usually a single, opaque color. If you don't use any other makeup, you should at least put on base!

BLEND: The action of smoothing one color of makeup into another color. This can require the use of a brush, a cotton swab, or something really sophisticated, like your fingers.

BLUSH/ROUGE: The red tint used to make your cheeks look rosy or tanned. The word "rouge" is French for *red*.

CHARACTER MAKEUP: A special makeup design used to *change* the actor's face. This is the opposite of *Straight Makeup*.

CREPE HAIR: Artificial hair made of wool fibers. It is the least expensive type of fake hair and is usually sold by the inch in tight braids at your local theatrical supply house. One inch contains three to five inches of hair when straightened.

DERMA WAX/NOSE PUTTY: Both of these are used to mold scars, noses, almost anything you need. Derma Wax was originally designed for undertakers and will not hold up long at body temperature. Nose putty is a bit more permanent but still becomes soft at warm temperatures.

EYEDROPPER: You know what this is, but its uses can be really strange. My husband uses it for applications of stage blood, making blisters in latex, and various sick-looking effects. You will probably get pretty good use out of it too!

EYELINER: The stuff you put around your eyes. It comes in pencils and in liquid form, as well as a variety of colors.

FALSE TEETH: Not the dental kind, the theatrical kind! These include those monster teeth you bought as a kid, as well as those nice, five-hundred-dollar jobs you saw at the last Star Trek convention.

FIXATIVE A: A clear, gluelike substance that seals latex pieces, nose putty constructs, and other semipermanent materials so that makeup can be applied to it more easily.

HAIR SPRAYS: This includes styling sprays, color sprays to alter the actor's hair color, and even sealant sprays used on artificial hair.

HIGHLIGHT: The reflected light on a surface above a dark wrinkle or the highest point of the facial area. In makeup these are usually painted on.

LIQUID LATEX: This substance normally comes in bottles or jars and sits in a makeup kit for years before it hardens and gets thrown out. It actually serves a lot of uses in building false noses or scars (like Derma Wax or nose putty) and in building your own reusable beards and mustaches.

MAKEUP REMOVER: A must for any actor. This includes petroleum jellies, cold creams, rubbing alcohol, baby wipes, and of course, *soap and water!*

PROSTHESIS: Anything you are gluing or fastening to your face or body, such as noses, horns, hair, or false wounds.

RIGID COLLODION: Originally designed as a glue, **rigid collodion** is a clear substance that shrinks as it dries. When it is applied to the skin, it shrinks up, causing the skin beneath to pucker. It works well in making scars.

RUBBER MASK SEALER: A clear liquid substance that allows latex to accept almost any kind of makeup or paint.

RUBBING ALCOHOL: The nice way to remove a prosthesis. The other way is just to pull real hard.

SHADOW: The opposite of **highlight.** Shadows are used in wrinkles or recessed areas of the face, such as the temples, beneath the chin, or around the eyes, as in **eye shadow.**

SPIRIT GUM/MEDICAL ADHESIVE: These adhesives are used to hold prostheses on to the face or body. **Spirit gum** is stronger, but it is not completely colorless and can cause reactions in sensitive skin types. **Medical adhesive** is clear and mostly hypoallergenic but is not quite as strong.

STAGE BLOOD: This is what we use when we want to reuse the actors. It is highly visible, usually made of corn syrup, red dye, and glycerine. Different companies make their own formulas, and some do not wash out of costumes. There are also different types of **stage blood,** such as liquid blood, blood capsules that are used to give the appearance of blood flowing from the mouth, blood bags that simulate bleeding by bursting them onstage, and my favorite, thick blood, a simulated congealed blood that really looks gross!

STIPPLE: The motion of touching a color on briefly and repeatedly in an up and down motion to create tiny "dots." This is used to make a week's growth of beard, or tiny blood vessels in a drunk's nose, or for a thousand other uses.

STIPPLE SPONGE: A sponge made of coarse fiber used to make dots when stippling. The term *sponge* is misleading; *it does not absorb!*

STRAIGHT MAKEUP: A makeup design not to disguise the actor, but to enhance and even "improve" the actor's looks. The most basic of all makeup designs.

TEXAS DIRT/PLAINS DUST: Clay-based powders used to tint the skin to dark tones or to simulate dirt onstage.

THEATRICAL TISSUE: The backstage term for the most universal of all substances: toilet paper. There are more uses for this than I have room to discuss in this book, and it comes in those handy rolls too!

TOOTH CRAYONS: Wax-based color that can tint your teeth all kinds of colors. The black ones are great for making missing teeth . . . just don't try eating with it on!

WIG CAP: This refers both to the mesh or rubber base that the wig is built on, and to the elasticized cap you can buy to hold your hair up beneath a wig.

CHAPTER 2

WHAT'S FIRST?

The most important part of your makeup is the base. If you have a flat tire on the way to the performance, forget doing anything else, but get your base on! Base is the first thing you put on; it's what makes you show up. It is the *foundation* for everything you put on your face. **Your base must be designed for the theatre. Purchase it from a theatrical makeup company!** Why, do you ask? Theatrical makeup bases are more opaque than regular makeup and stop light at the surface of the skin. Over-the-counter, or "street makeup," foundations allow light to penetrate and natural skin color to show through. Street makeups are not dense enough for the stage.

There are three different types of bases: *grease, pancake, and cream. Greasepaint* is a petroleum-based product (you might have guessed by the name) originally made from dry pigment and rendered ham fat. Obviously that nice bacon smell didn't go unnoticed, and actors today are still affectionately called "hams." The best reason to look for grease is for the unusual and bright colors that may not be found in other types of bases. Grease is also good for covering Derma Wax and latex pieces or masks. Grease is very flexible (like oil painting on the skin), but it is also very heavy and must be removed with a cold cream type of cleanser. *Note: Grease does not dry, ever! It must be held in place with a light application of translucent facial powder.*

Pancake is a water-based makeup that needs to be applied with a damp sponge. Once it is dry it does not require powder to hold it on. It is removable with soap and water.

Cream will come in a variety of colors, can be applied and removed easily, but has a much more limited shelf life than the other two. Cream might be considered the middle ground between grease and pancake makeup.

When choosing your base, consider the following: What type of skin do you have, and what does the part you are playing require? Sometimes the role will dictate what kind of makeup you choose. For example, if you are playing a different race, an animal, or a clown, you will need to make sure your base will cover well and be opaque. For most actors, the aim is to build a makeup kit that is face-friendly. Know your skin type and how to care for it. If you have dry skin, a cream might be better. If you have oily skin, go for the pancake.

OK, you have selected a base that looks and feels right on you. What else do you need? Just a few other essentials before you start.

HEY! WHAT'S IN THE TACKLE BOX?

To the unlearned eye it appears to be an average tackle box, shoe box, or lunch pail. But for the actor, it's *magic!* This tiny box holds the elemental formulas to turn you into . . .

Here's what you need to start with: Your base foundation, eyeliner/brow pencil, cheek color, lip color, and powder. (If you are using a pancake base, you can skip the powder.) If you normally play a "straight" character, this will be enough. Any of these items may be purchased at a theatrical supply house or makeup company. However, **except for the base,** you can locate them in a drugstore. You should also look into student kits available at most theatrical supply houses. They are usually reasonable in price, the items are within specific color ranges, and have everything you need plus a few extras.

As stated earlier, the **base** is very important. It should be a color that closely matches your own skin. You might try buying small containers to start with while you are still learning. The reason be-

CONTENTS OF A STANDARD MAKEUP KIT: ① MAKEUP BASES (CREAM, GREASE, OR PANCAKE.) AND A SPONGE. ② EYEBROW PENCILS. ③ LIQUID EYELINER. ④ POWDER, PETROLEUM JELLY, THEATRICAL TISSUE (TOILET PAPER). ⑤ CREAM OR DRY ROUGE, PENCIL SHARPENER, COTTON SWABS, A LARGE MAKEUP BRUSH. ⑥ ALCOHOL OR MAKEUP REMOVER, POWDER PUFF. ⑦ COTTON BALLS, TOOTHBRUSH. ⑧ EYE SHADOW COLORS AND SMALL MAKEUP BRUSHES.

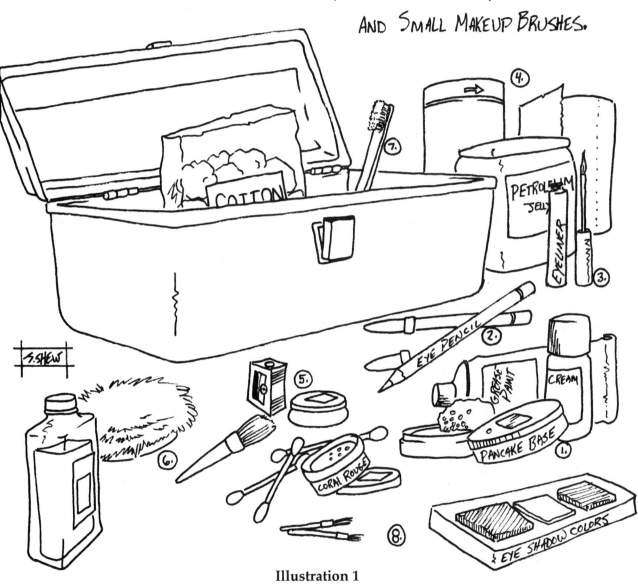

Illustration 1

ing that sometimes a color will match your skin, but not look right onstage. You might need a shade darker or lighter. You may also decide whether you like cream bases or pancake, or find you need a hypoallergenic base. Don't buy a huge amount of anything until you know what works for you.

Eyeliner/brow pencils should be in colors that complement your skin tone. Color guidelines: If you are fair to light brown in coloring, use a light brown pencil. Redheads can use a medium or a dark brown pencil. Brunettes or darker colored skin tones can use a black pencil. If you have white hair and eyebrows try a medium gray or "charcoal" for an eyeliner color. You'll find several shades of pencils and may want more than one.

Cheek and lip color might be the same item for some people. If you like being really thrifty and the technique works for you, this is one thing less to buy. You can use powdered or cream blushes (also called rouge), but you should be aware that a cream formulated for your face will be heavier and might be too harsh for your lips. Still, you can experiment. Mix a little cream rouge with petroleum jelly and apply it to your lips. If you use a powder-based cheek color and want to try it on your lips, a little petroleum jelly applied to the lips first will help hold it in place. For cheek and lip color I usually guide men toward the russet or brown tones, and women toward the red or pink. Again, try to find a color that looks natural on you.

Powder usually comes in a few skin tone colors or in pale pink. Any of these will probably work, as they are translucent and mostly serve to set your makeup. If you need to, you can also use white baby powder. Check the prices on powder before you buy. Quantity and color may vary widely from drugstores to theatrical supply houses. **Do not make the mistake of buying Texas Dirt or Plains Dust to use as a powder!** These are actually clay-based products used to tint the skin, and they do not work the same way as facial powder.

Other helpful tools to keep in your magic box will be: **cotton swabs, small makeup brushes, a large brush for powder, cotton balls, sponges, shadow colors, a pencil sharpener, clothespins, bobby pins, rubbing alcohol, a toothbrush** for adding streaks in a beard or graying eyebrows, **facial cleansers,** and **theatrical tissue** (aka: toilet paper). (See illustration 1.)

WHO AM I, AND WHAT DO I LOOK LIKE?

Before you get out your makeup kit, you must have some idea in mind of how your character looks. Some clues to the character's appearance will be given in the script, the director will have definite ideas, and sometimes the cast members have suggestions. But you must know your character well enough to make judgments about his or her appearance. After all, **you're the one inside.** What you put on the outside will only enhance what you've already created.

In discussing appearance for the first time, you'll probably want to think in broad terms of costume and makeup to create a total, finished look. Also, don't forget that the way you walk, talk, and gesture are part of the visual perception. These are acting areas, but they can influence your appearance too. You may need to take some care in selecting your makeup and costume in regards to the physical attributes you choose. If you need to walk with a limp, make sure your costume allows you to do that.

What factors influence appearance? The most fundamental element will be the body itself: height, weight, sex, race, and age. These are things you can't change a great deal, but with costume and makeup they are factors that can be enhanced or diminished slightly. Other influences on appearance will be: time period of the play, culture of the character, character's occupation, lifestyle, health, and wealth.

The best place to start looking for clues is in the script. The playwright had a personality in mind when the play was written, and there is usually a cursory description on the cast of characters page. Also, while you're reading the play, take the time to make notes. What specific information is in the text? Look for what the character says about himself, what others say, what the playwright includes in parentheses.

After a few rehearsals, talk with your director. He might not have specific details in mind yet, but he will probably be envisioning a type of personality, general appearance, and a few clothing ideas. Listen to what other cast members say. If you're hearing a repeated comment, it probably means you've done such a good acting job that you're creating a visual image of the character for them already. Run your ideas by the director first, though, to make sure everyone is of the same mind. One sketch I directed recently had a flamboyant character that *everyone* in the cast visualized in a turban. Obviously, that's what we had the actress wear! It intensified her character and the way the other actors related to her. Remember, acting is 90% **internal;** costume and makeup just **enhance** the process.

Let's create a character. ("Igor, the vial, please!") Let's say your character is a woman from the 1890s. To start with, we might *assume* a prairie look, but does she live in the Midwest, the East Coast, or the Pacific Northwest? This will directly influence your costume. What time of year is it? Being outside in the winter will indicate a different costume from summer outdoor wear. Does she live in town, or is she from a rural area? Is the character on the farm with a little sunburn and ground-in dirt, or are there enough ranch hands, slaves, or servants that our lady doesn't really get soiled? How does she wear her hair? If she's on the farm, it needs to be out of the way and simple. If she's in town working at the dress store, she would take a little more time with it, maybe she would wear a small jewel for interest. Is she matronly with a few children, unmarried, a new bride, an older spinster? These all conjure up mental images, don't they?

At least by now you're visualizing general costume, bearing, and personality types possible. Facial makeup should be a final touch to this general image. If she's the wife of a poor dirt farmer and they're not eating too well, her face will reflect that: A few "worry" lines, a little sunburn, less color in the cheeks and lips, her hair pulled back and a little wispy, her cheeks a little sunken. Do you see her yet?

Now, let's take our unfortunate lady out of the Kansas dust storms and say she's married to a ship baron in New England. You have a general idea already; she has better clothing, she probably stays at home with the servants, and she's well-fed. She'll be pale but rosy. Her hair is shiny and well put up, perhaps in a decorative braid. Allow for fullness and color in the cheeks and lips, and not too many lines on her untroubled brow. All this and no script! See what you can do!

THE BASIC FACE (Everybody Has One)

This is called basic or straight makeup because there's nothing fancy about it. You just want to show up under the lights. So take your clean face and your base of choice and start putting them together. Make sure you wash your face before you start, to remove any dirt or old makeup. If you are using grease or cream base, splash cool water on your skin to help close the pores, then pat dry. (Rubbing irritates the skin.)

Before you start, let me throw out two ideas: *more is better* and *darker is better*. Now that I've thrown them out, *you throw them out too!* Both of them belong in the trash! Another myth I'd trash is "this will wash out." It never does! Put on the costume after the makeup. If it has to go on over your head, put it on first and drape a towel over it while you do makeup.

I always start from the top of the face and work down. If your base is a cream, use your fingers or a sponge to apply it. If you use a water-soluble or pancake base, you'll need a sponge and some water. Be careful not to put too much water in the sponge, or your face will run. (Definitely not pretty!) Be sure to blend carefully, taking the color up into the hairline (however far back that may be) and under the jaw line into the neck area. Be careful to blend slowly and smoothly down the neck if you have a costume to consider. Pay special attention to the eye area, around the nose, and your ears. These areas have a lot of creases and hollows that tend to get missed, leaving white spots that look bad under the lights. If you are using a pancake base, you will notice it looks very splotchy when it first goes on. Allow it to dry before doing any touch-ups. It will dry much smoother. (See illustration 2a.)

Next, go for the eyes! (Don't worry; it's not that scary!) Use a brow pencil to darken or extend the brows if necessary. Use short strokes and follow the directions in which the hair grows. You will be darkening the hair as well as some of the skin underneath. Now comes the hard part for most people, lining the eyes. Use whatever is comfortable for you, liquid or pencil. I prefer pencil because I like the control and durability. Start at the inside corner and come to the outside of the eye on the upper lid at the base of the lashes. Now do the same under the lower lashes. That wasn't so bad, was it? The difficulty for anyone is that the eye area is very sensitive. Be very careful and go slowly until you are used to the sensation. You may find that your eyes will water; stop and wait until the watering stops. If you wear contacts, decide what works best for you: doing your eyes before or after you put them in. (See illustration 2b.)

Next you may wish to add eye shadow or mascara. If you have deep-set eyes, a lighter color can help them be seen more. If your face is too "flat" under light, use a darker shadow to help define the

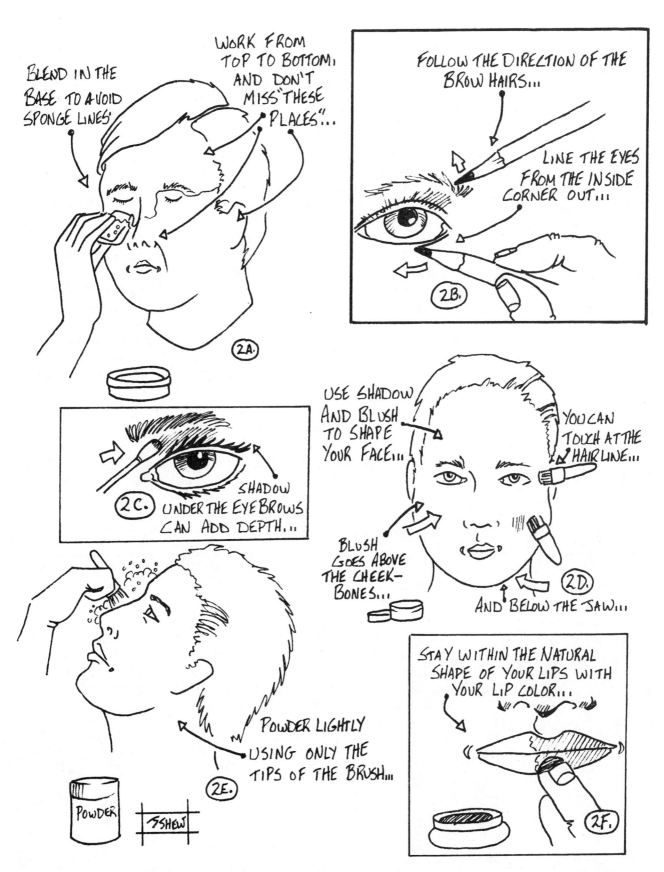

eye area. The use of shadow with straight makeup is not so much to "go with your outfit" but to help you appear normal under stage lights. Quite often the use of mascara is not that effective from stage, but I don't discourage actors from using it. It's that "mental boost" theory again. (See illustration 2c.)

If you would like to try false lashes for effect, *be careful.* They look nice if you get them large enough to be seen from stage. The difficulty is getting them on and off. Read instructions well and always practice ahead of time. It's easy to get lash adhesive in your eye, or pull out your real lashes! *Never use any type of adhesive with false lashes that isn't made for them. You risk damage to the lashes and your eyes!*

Now for a little color. Everyone needs a little cheek color in order to look natural. For straight makeup, always stay within your normal skin tones. Blush goes on the upper side of the cheekbones, toward the temples. You may also want to hit the hairline, chin, or jawline, but lightly. You can use blush in this way to contour or add dimension to your face. You may also use a shadow color to do the same thing, usually a shade of brown. If you have a small nose, use a little shadow down the sides of the nose to help. Is your face round? Try shadowing at the jawline and blend into the neck. Maybe a shadow at the temples or under the cheek is what you need. Experiment! (See illustration 2d.)

Next, powder if necessary. If you've used any cream shadows or a cream or grease base, you will need a light dusting to hold everything in place. If you are using pancake and powder-based makeup, you should be all right without the powder fixative. To apply powder, use a large brush or a puff. Dip the brush or puff into the powder and tap off the excess. Pat the powder on lightly, don't rub. You can always put on more if you need to, but a "blob" of powder is very hard to remove. If you use a brush, only the very tips of the bristles should be dipped into the powder and stipple your face, or you'll get brush strokes! Stippling is a bouncing motion in a straight line, done very gently to just touch the brush tips to your face. **Note:** Be careful that you don't breathe the powder into your lungs. (See illustration 2e.)

If you perspire heavily during a performance, try starting with a water-based makeup. It won't "move" as readily as cream, and you can dry the sweat by using a towel to blot (don't rub) your face as the performance progresses.

Don't forget to put some lips on! (Men usually gripe about this, but they get over it.) The mouth and the eyes are the most important parts of facial communication! Use a color that is within the normal skin tones. Women can usually get away with a more vibrant color if they are playing a modern character. To apply lip color, use your finger, a lip brush, or regular lipstick. Stay within the normal lines of the lips. You may want to use a little powder, applied with a cotton ball, to hold it better. (See illustration 2f.)

That's it! Your straight makeup is complete! Now, **this is very important: You must have someone look at you under the stage lights!** If at all possible, the lights should be gelled and focused as they will be for performance. What they are looking for is: **from the middle of the audience space, does your face look normal and do you show up?** Is it too dark or too light? Is it too "flat" looking? Is there too great a color difference between your hands and your face? Do you need to put base on your hands? Does your neck match your face? Did you miss areas altogether with your base, leaving "hot spots"? Dress rehearsal is the time to fix all these little problems. Now, practice, practice, practice! Practice will help you gain speed, skill, and confidence. You'll learn what works well on your skin and what products you like best. Knowing your face and its problems will help you work under adverse conditions; such as when your makeup room is a mirror nailed to a tree!

CHAPTER 3

MIDDLE AGE AND OLD AGE

From straight makeup to middle age is not so great a leap. It's surprising what a few lines on your face can do. (You can hardly wait, you say?) The area around the eyes and the labial folds around the mouth (those lines that run from the side of your nose to the corners of your mouth) are the first prominent signs of middle age. (See illustration 3a.) Use a brow pencil to enhance these. Darken inside the crease, then add a white highlight in either cream or pencil and blend it enough so that from the audience it doesn't look like someone just drew lines on your face. (Although that's exactly what we just did!) Now try a little shadow at the temples to recess them a bit (make them look a little sunken).

Now add a little contour with shadow at the jawline. Most folks will start to lose facial elasticity in middle age, and there begins to be a slight sagging at the jaw. How about those first gray hairs starting to creep in? You can see them, but most of the hair still has its color. You might try a color hair spray, but I suggest a toothbrush with a little white makeup. This will give you a little more control over how heavy the color gets. This technique is good if the character ages slowly through the play. (See illustration 3b.)

Before we get any older, let's talk about **Highlight, Shadow,** and **Blending.** Highlight and shadow go together to create **dimension** in everything we see. We see the shadow *because* of the light. (That sounds religious or something . . .) Anyway, the more wrinkles you want to create, the more you shadow and highlight. **An important rule for creating highlight and shadow: Lines running in a vertical path must be highlighted** *from the nose outward toward the temples.* **Lines in a horizontal path must be highlighted** *on the top of the shadow.* This idea stems from looking at a person onstage. Light comes from overhead and spills to the side of the face. (See Illustration 3c.) **Another rule to remember is that** *highlight is the reflected light on those areas that are protruding. Shadow is found in the areas that are receding.* The same is true for color; light colors are *forward,* dark colors are *back.* Blending is important and takes practice. Remember, all you want to do is smooth one color of makeup into another color. You don't want to look like you have lines drawn on your face, but the opposite of that is blending so much that you lose all definition, leaving you with a muddy, blurred look.

Now, let's make you older. At this point you may have to make a decision about your character to finish the look you want. Is the character heavy or thin? In good health or poor? These factors can influence the color of the skin. It might be clear, slightly yellow, or covered with a lot of broken veins just below the surface, which create dark rings under the eyes, a red nose, or other unattractive features. Wrinkles begin to appear in the forehead. These can be done with a pencil and highlighted. Brown age spots appear; they can be added with a brown pencil (as long as it's dull) or a medium brown cream and a brush. Remember: They are random. Don't make them too uniform in color, size, or shape. (See illustration 3d.) Eyes recess into the skull. You can achieve this by using a darker shadow in the crease of the eyelid, then use a highlight on the brow bone. You will need to try above or below the eyebrow, depending on your facial shape. Try a shadow below the cheekbone to give that sunken appearance. (That also means you will have to highlight on *top of the bone.*) In men, the facial bones begin to "sharpen" with age, giving most of them a hard look. Experiment with the top of the bone and highlight to make an almost definite edge. Also, with age the lips begin to lose some of

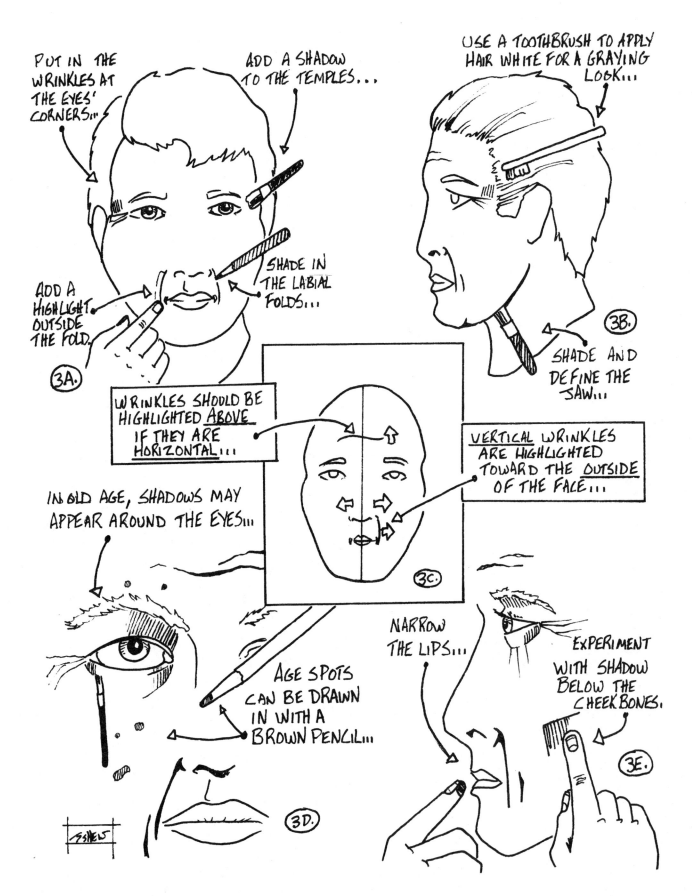

their fullness. Use a little base color to "pull in" the edges of the lip line and make the lips appear thinner. (See illustration 3e.)

RACIAL MAKEUP (And Now, for Something Completely Different . . .)

You probably won't need to portray other races often, but it's a challenge you may want to try. There are a few things you have to think about to pull this off with style: If you do this the wrong way, it will be distracting and possibly insulting. Your makeup should be done very well, as should your hair. By the time you are doing the makeup, you should have already immersed yourself in the culture, history, beliefs, social behavior, body movements, and speech patterns of the race you wish to portray. **Acting will be crucial, don't depend on a good makeup job to cover a bad accent.**

Start your makeup with the mental checklist. What do you know about the character's age, social standing, lifestyle, etc.? Then I suggest you do some serious observation of people around you of that race, and start collecting pictures to work from. Keep your own face in mind; what characteristics are going to be problems for you? Will you need a wig? A nose piece? A different base color?

Don't make the mistake of thinking "they all look alike." Everyone has a slightly different tone of skin, face shape, eye shape, or what have you. You can use these subtle differences to help create variety in your character.

As always, the base color will be most important. Even more important: **complete coverage!** Be sure to look out for areas you don't normally do; behind the ears, back of the neck, front of the neck into the chest area, hands and arms. *If it shows at any time, put makeup on it!*

To select a base, I suggest going to a theatrical supply house and getting a salesperson to help you choose. This means not only the right racial group but the right *tone*. For example, if your character is East Indian, you have a range of tones from coffee and cream, to deep olive, to almost red. Pick a color that will most fit your tone—fair, medium, or dark. Now choose colors to complement your base for the liners, cheek and lip color. **Note:** Go ahead and cover your lips in the base color, this will help keep your natural color from altering your *chosen* lip color.

Hair color and style are important; don't cheat your illusion by neglecting this area. For minimal fuss, try using hats, turbans, or whatever covering would be acceptable for the culture and time period. But don't do it to everyone in the cast—that can be boring. Color changes can be done with rinses, sprays, or wigs. In some cases a wig is the best choice—certain styles and/or colors may be too drastic. **Warning:** If you have light brown, blond, or white hair, *do not* color your hair with the idea it will wash out. Fair hair absorbs color like a sponge. It will grow out, but not wash out. (See illustration 4.)

PLANTS, ANIMALS, AND THINGS THAT GO BUMP IN THE NIGHT

Such as monsters, clowns, aliens, phantoms, and the X-Men. This is a fun, creative, pull-out-all-the-stops area. Try anything! It's in this area that artificial pieces usually come onto your face, but for our beginners let's keep that to a minimum and use mostly makeup.

I suggest a brainstorm session first to get your basic ideas on paper before you start. Copy the makeup chart included, and with colored pencils make a few sketches of what you would like to look like. This will save time, supplies, and wear on your face. Also make notes on your costume, hair, hands, and feet so that your character will have a "finished" look about it. Keep the same level of detail in all the elements. It can be distracting to have a finely detailed makeup job and a so-so costume. If you are limited in budget or time, keep it all simple.

An easy start in this area might be a clown. And no, you don't have to use greasepaint! Try a cream base; use the traditional white or pick a wild color! You can use one or more colors for a base, rather than layering colors, which might dilute their intensity. To create some details, try colored eyeliners, cream colors applied with a small brush, or liquid eyeliners. A black liquid eyeliner is a handy item for any fantasy makeup; it's great for outlining colored areas or for creating solid lines and details. While you are learning, don't try for too much detail or too many colors. Otherwise all those pretty colors will run together into "sludge" very quickly!

Animals are fun both for the makeup and the acting challenge. For ideas, go to the zoo, look at books and nature shows. Kids' coloring books are good sources for critters too. When designing an animal face, make sure the complexity is in line with the overall feel of the performance. Meaning: Does the play require it to be cartoonish or more realistic? (See illustration 5.)

MAKEUP DESIGN SHEET

SHOW_____

CHARACTER___ASIAN MALE_____

ACTOR___JOE ANYBODY_____

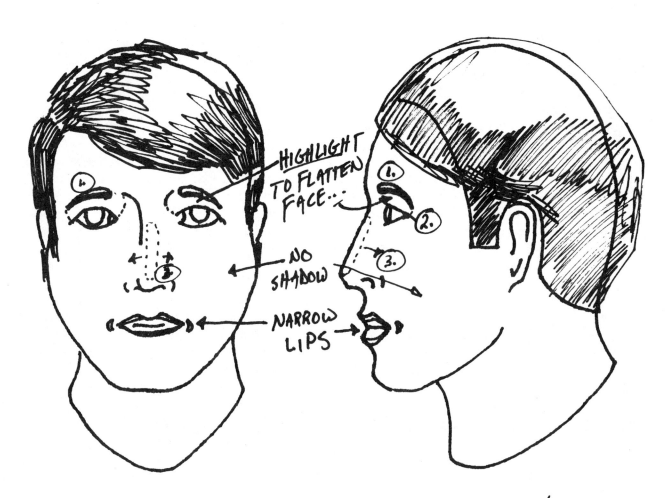

BASE _ASIAN "V2"_   EYE SHADOW _WHITE / YELLOW_

PENCIL/LINER _BLACK_____   HIGHLIGHT _WHITE (CHEEKS, EYES)_

ROUGE _CORAL (LIGHT!)_   LIP COLOR _PALE_____

HAIR _BLACK, COMB STRAIGHT_____

NOTES

① NARROW EYEBROWS, ② ADD ANGLES TO EYES, FLATTEN FACE.
BE VERY CAREFUL WITH SHADOW & HIGHLIGHT
③ HIGHLIGHT ON NOSE BRIDGE, BLEND OUTWARD!

MAKEUP DESIGN SHEET

SHOW _____

CHARACTER "DOGGY" HOUND DOG... _____

ACTOR _____ Suzy CHILDSTAR _____

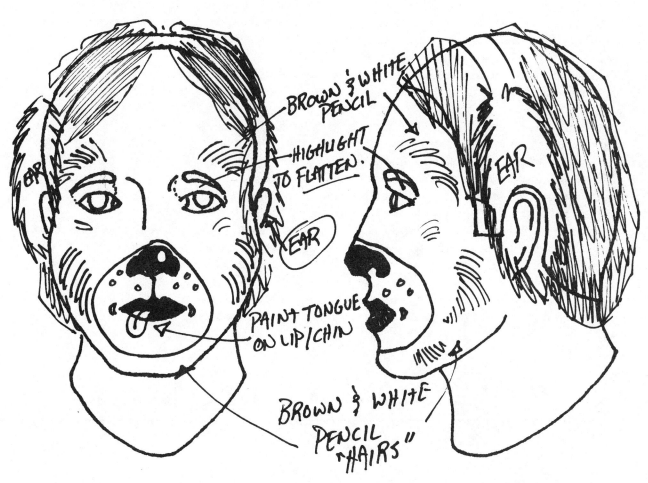

BASE _BROWN / LIGHT BROWN_   EYE SHADOW _HIGHLIGHT_

PENCIL/LINER _BROWN / WHITE_   HIGHLIGHT _WHITE_

ROUGE _N/A_   LIP COLOR _BLACK_

HAIR _(ADD DOG EARS ON HEADBAND_

NOTES

"MUZZLE" IS LIGHT BROWN/TAN. PAINT NOSE & MOUTH BLACK.

"TONGUE" IS RED, PAINTED ON. HANG "DOG EARS" FROM

HEADBAND. REST OF FACE MED/DARK BROWN w/ HAIRS of PENCIL

For other fantastic beings, start with simple ideas first—just being a bright blue person can be fun! Do an off-the-wall color for a base, then do the rest of your face as if you're doing straight make-up for a person with that skin tone. Try *simple* additions to your face, such as a clown nose, a little Derma Wax or nose putty. Make a wart, add some whiskers, a little crepe hair here or there, or a pre-made latex nose or scar. As before, make sure to design with the finished look of your character in mind.

Anytime you start gluing things to your face you must remember to **leave that area free of makeup.** You can do touch-ups after everything is in place. **Important Note: Be very careful around your eyes, nose, and mouth.** Your mucous membranes are very sensitive and the last place you want to damage.

There are three types of adhesives you can use on your skin (artificial nail adhesive is *not* one of them). The three types are **spirit gum, medical adhesive,** and **eyelash adhesive.** Spirit gum is a little more harsh on the skin than medical adhesive, but both work well for holding on latex pieces, lumps of Derma Wax, or nose putty. Spirit gum is stronger and can last longer than medical adhesive, but it is not entirely clear. Medical adhesive is not only clear but less likely to cause allergic reactions. You won't find spirit gum or medical adhesive in a drugstore; go to your theatre shop. Medical adhesive is actually used in surgical procedures to temporarily hold things in place prior to stitches. Both types of glue can be removed using a cotton ball soaked in rubbing alcohol. Allow the alcohol to seep under the item to be removed and pull gently at it, one edge at a time. Easy does it!

Eyelash adhesive is sold wherever you find false lashes. Its not as heavy duty as the other two, but it works fine with lightweight items such as sequins, feathers, small warts, or eyelashes. This glue can be gently pulled off the skin, and any makeup remover will get rid of the rest.

When using Derma Wax, keep in mind that it doesn't hold up for long periods or under high heat. It's actually designed for morticians to use on bodies, which are usually cold. Nose putty is a little sturdier, and if you coat it with fixative, it will make it somewhat reusable, but not bulletproof.

CHAPTER 4

HAIR AND WIGS

Hair falls somewhere between the categories of makeup and costume. For some, it just falls out in the sink. But it's definitely important to the total, finished look of your character. Anytime you see a period play or movie, look at the way they've treated the hair, head gear, and facial hair. Too often this area is neglected, causing the viewer to be distracted. Your brain has a way of saying "what's wrong with this picture?" and you don't even realize you are distracted until you notice you've missed the dialogue. A well-thought-out design takes these areas into consideration.

Although your hair may be a modern style, and you're doing a modern play, is your hair in the *right style for the character?* A different hairstyle can make a world of difference in the way a person looks. Sometimes, simply combing a man's hair off his face to reveal the hairline will create the illusion of middle age. Women are much less structured in their fashions and hair designs, therefore *more* attention to style is required to visually enhance the character. By this I mean there have been so many styles throughout history that you should be careful what you choose to do with your hair, and don't neglect to do research. Men's hair and clothing has typically been more conservative with slight alterations—they can slide by a little easier!

Let's talk about coloring your hair. (I said *talk;* don't do anything rash yet!) First of all, don't do it unless you really have to. Second, wigs might be the better choice. The most obvious reasons to change hair color are **age** and **race**. Age is easier to deal with—everyone will go gray, white, or silver at some point. To estimate what your hair will tend toward, look at the parent you favor in coloring now (this won't work if you're adopted). **Blonds** tend to go white more smoothly because there is less pigment to start with. The transition is less noticeable. **Medium brown to dark**-haired persons have the most contrast. **Redheads** tend to get a bum deal—they seem to fade into a peach or pink shade before a final stage is reached.

For different races, make sure you really need to change color first. Do a little research. Not all the Irish are redheads, not all Italians are dark, and not all Scandinavians are towheads. Sometimes a very slight change will be enough to carry the effect from a distance. Two shades lighter or darker might do the trick. If a **radical change from your own hair color is needed, look into all your options** first. You can use a number of commercial sprays, rinses, tinted shampoos, or have it professionally dyed. Do some wig shopping too.

Be aware before you do anything: Blond hair **absorbs** color—no, it will not wash out! If you need to portray age, use a *white* spray—that's the safest thing to do. A silver or gray color will give your natural blond hair a dull gray look even after washing. For other colors, consider having your hair *professionally* dyed and then redyed after the performance (I'd warn people at work). If you decide to go that route, be sure to have them do your eyebrows to match, facial hair, too, if needed. Or use wigs to get a darker color. *If your hair is already colored or permed, **please** have it **professionally** colored or use wigs.*

I usually leave hair until the makeup is done. Have the person gently cover his or her face with a towel to protect it, spray the hair, then do touch-ups to the makeup as needed. If hair has to be rinsed with color, do that first. Blot it dry and allow for time to dry before doing costume and makeup. If it's required that the actor has a specific hairstyle and color, I recommend styling first, then spray on the color.

To use a spray, apply a little and brush it into the hair first. Then do a final "top coat" spray. I recommend purchasing a **theatrical quality spray** rather than a Halloween-type. Those types don't have staying power; they tend to glob and flake off quickly. If you just need a little color around the hairline, or a streaked look, use a small brush, or even a toothbrush. Spray color into it and apply to hair. Pancake makeup can be used in the hair as well, although it's not as long lasting.

Wigs, of course, come in many different styles, colors, and prices. You can always find cheap Halloween-style wigs. Synthetic hair wigs are somewhat steeper in price, and natural hair wigs are always the most expensive. You will have to decide what will work best for you. If the character will be wearing a head drape or a hat, a cheap wig works just fine. Cheap wigs can also be used later for the hair fibers to create mustaches or beards. **Hint: If possible, buy wigs in the off season (summer) or just after Halloween is over.** You might also check in thrift stores, and a lot of people are more than happy to donate old wigs. If you need something in the specialty line (such as powdered wigs, geisha style, sumo wrestler, punk haircuts, etc.), ask at your local theatrical costume shops, and be prepared to spend some cash.

Once you've acquired the wig you need, you want to take care of it. If you've purchased it in a thrift store or it was donated, you definitely want to wash the wig before wearing it.

If the wig is very long or tangled, comb through it gently before washing it. (See illustration 6a.) You should expect to lose some hair out of the wig, but be patient, don't rip it out by the handful like you would your own. **Wig hair does not grow back.** Wash the wig in an apple-based shampoo, or purchase a wig shampoo. I've also used a *mild* clothing detergent, or mild dish soap. In a sink of cool water, swish the wig through the water enough to get it wet, then gently work a lather into it. Now, allow it to soak for a while. After about 15 minutes (or during a commercial break), rinse the wig in cool water, thoroughly! Any leftover detergent can irritate the scalp. After a nice rinse, gently squeeze the excess water from the wig. *Don't wring it!* (See illustration 6b.)

Lay the wig on a towel. Roll up the towel starting at the ends of the hair. Again, gently squeeze the wig inside the towel. If the wig is very thick, or long haired, "sandwich" it between two towels and roll it up. (See illustration 6c.)

After you've squeezed it to death, put it over a large can (i.e., a one pound coffee can) to dry. This will allow circulation of air throughout the wig and the wig cap (that's the elastic area where the hair is attached). *Do not comb wigs when they're wet!* You will only stretch the hair fibers, causing it to be "frizzy," and you'll lose a lot more hair in the process. This rule goes for natural hair wigs too. For very long wigs, I suggest a wig conditioner. Spray it on, and after it dries, brush it through to help prevent tangling. (See illustration 6d.)

After washing and air drying, your wig should have resumed its original style. A gentle combing should be enough to make it presentable. If this is not the case, you have more work ahead of you. Rewet the hair (I use a spray bottle), and use plastic or sponge rollers and allow the hair to air dry again. Then comb and restyle. Yes, you will want to invest in a good wig stand, or a very patient person to sit with the wig on while you style. (I've used both. Trust me; **buy a wig stand!**) (See illustration 6e.)

Important: Do not use steam, curling irons, or blow dryers; avoid heat altogether when styling wigs. Synthetic hair can be melted, or at the very least become brittle and break off. Natural hair is made of protein and will dry out, become brittle, and break. Natural hair also burns easily and smells awful!

To keep a wig in place on your head, you must first secure your own hair. If you have short hair, you're better off. A bobby pin or two will probably do the job. If you have medium to long hair, try the following tricks and see what works best for you: (1) Pull the hair up on top and secure with bobby pins; (2) "wrap" your hair around your head and secure it with bobby pins; or (3) use a wig cap. (See Illustration 6f.) A wig cap is designed to be worn under wigs. It looks like a swimmer's cap made of elastic mesh. It helps you get a nice, smooth, no-bumps look before donning the wig. Keep in mind that an ill-fitting wig can cause you headaches. Practice getting your own hair to lay smooth underneath the wig.

After the performance is over, you may want to wash the wig before storing it. Store wigs on stands if you have them—it helps them keep their shape. You can also use a wadded-up ball of tissue paper in the wig cap, and curl the hair around itself in a box. Store them out of the light, *away from heat.*

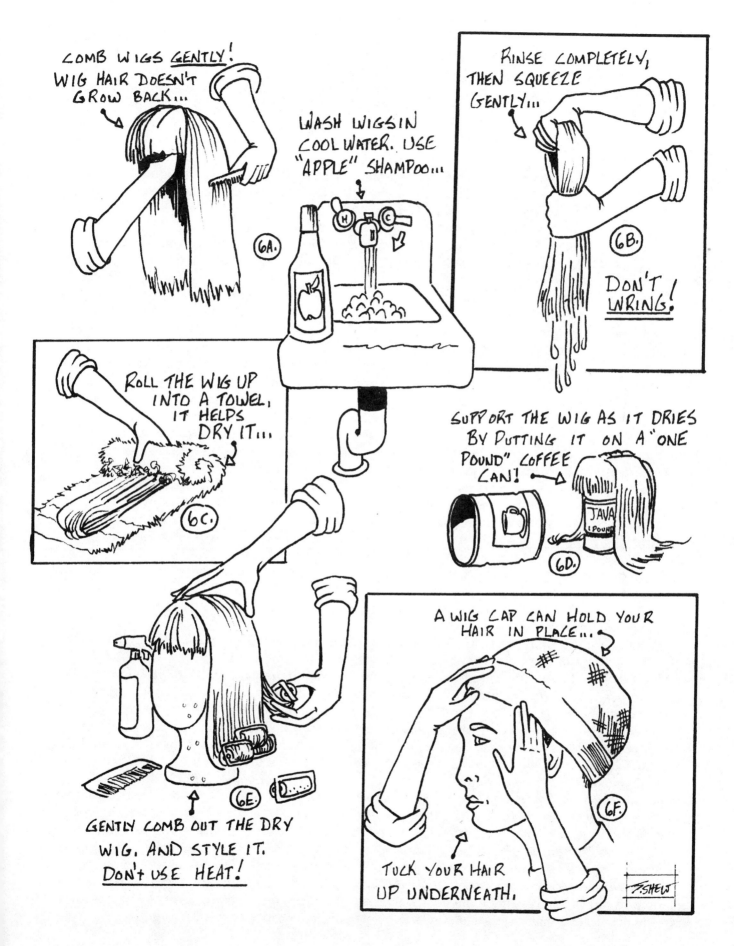

BEARDS AND MUSTACHES

At some point in time you'll probably find yourself in the middle of a pageant play trying to transform Mr. Clean-Cut-Accountant into . . . Moses! It won't be easy, but a beard might help. In dealing with facial hair for plays, my first suggestion is "grow your own!" However, in many professions this is not practical, and one must find a reasonable way around this problem.

Like wigs, beards and mustaches come in a great variety at your costume shop. All sizes, styles, colors, and prices. Reminder: A natural-looking beard is usually one or two shades darker than your head hair. The best quality beards are made of *synthetic or natural hair, hand-tied to a mesh backing.* These are applied to the face using *spirit gum* or *medical adhesive.* They last long, but can be expensive. A step down from that would be a beard that is *glued to a mesh backing.* There are also *premade latex-backed beards* (which I will teach you to make). Latex will not be as flexible or long-lived, but it's less expensive and can be very customized if you make your own.

Words of Wisdom: Making beards is a messy, time-consuming, and tricky process. It requires practice. Don't kick yourself if you really mess up the first one! If you do well the first time around, take yourself out to dinner!

To start preparation for beard making, get your *crepe hair* straightened first. Crepe hair is made of wool fibers and comes braided, with plenty of colors to choose from. It's usually sold by the half-foot or longer. A standard full beard can be done with six inches, crepe hair will stretch quite a bit in the straightening process. (You may wish to use it "curly" too, but buy a little more.) To straighten hair, cut lengths of a reasonable length, say three inches, and remove the braiding cord. In a container of warm (not hot) water, trail your strand of hair until it straightens. Lay them on a towel and blot them dry, allow them to air dry for a while before using. Then spread your strands out a little so you have smaller bunches of hair to work with. (See illustration 7a.)

OK—let's grow some hair on your face! Start by giving yourself a good close shave (hopefully without nicks), and *don't use aftershave.* Make sure to wash your face too. Allow your face to "rest" for about 15 to 20 minutes. Splash your face with a little cool water and pat it dry with a towel. This helps tighten the pores. If you're female and want to try this for grins, follow the same procedure (except the shaving part). Use *no* astringents or lotions.

Now we begin with a layer of liquid latex in the area you want to create the beard, mustache, or sideburns. Pour a small amount of latex into a container. Don't use too much; it dries out very quickly. Use a *disposable* makeup sponge dipped in the latex and spread evenly over the area. Allow this layer to dry completely, becoming clear. *Do not flex your face muscles* during this process, as that will dislodge the latex. (Don't watch comedians, or attempt this with a head cold.) Add a second layer in the same manner. To speed up drying, you can use a hair dryer set on low. These two layers become the foundation for the beard. (See illustration 7b.)

Begin to apply a third layer, but not all over the face yet; you must start adding the hair at this stage. *I do the beard area first, then the mustache because it grows over the beard.*

Start at the chin area first. Apply a little latex to the chin underneath (the hair grows *toward* the face here), add the hair *tips* in from back to front, stopping at the point of the chin. **Be very gentle, as the latex on this layer is not dry yet and the hair is easily dislodged.** Next, do the chin from the point up to the lip. The hair grows downward here. Once you've finished the chin area, start going up the sides of the face, layering the hair. The hair direction should be toward the chin and downward. Do your mustache too. (See illustration 7c.) When you feel you've created the "wolf man," it's about time to stop. **Note:** It's OK if the beard looks really shaggy at this point, you can trim it later when it's dry. *You must allow time for the latex to dry before doing anything else—around 30 to 45 minutes on the face.* After the latex has dried, you may trim the beard. If need dictates, the beard can be removed at this time and reattached later for trimming. I suggest trimming the beard while it is on the actor's face for best results. A more natural effect can be achieved by placing your hands on the beard and pressing lightly. This will cause the hair to curve down and under the actor's face. (See illustration 7d.)

After working with the combination of latex and crepe hair, you may fully expect to be covered in latex and tiny bits of hair, not to mention being tense and irritable. Rubbing alcohol will cure most of this, whether removing excess hair and latex from your hands, or getting a massage.

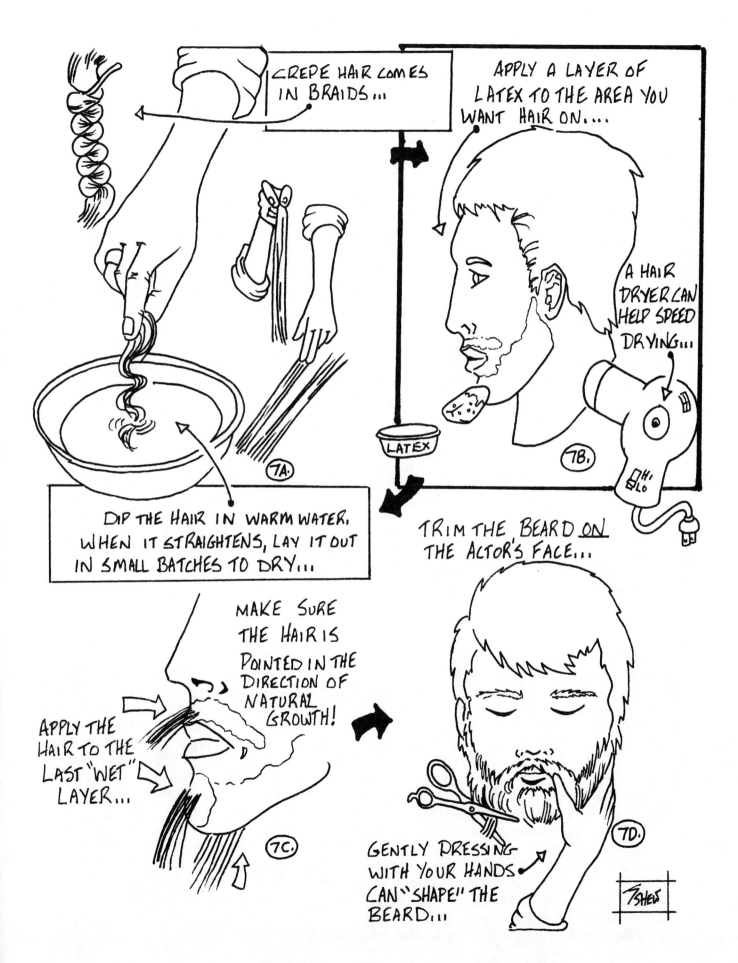

CREPE HAIR COMES IN BRAIDS...

APPLY A LAYER OF LATEX TO THE AREA YOU WANT HAIR ON...

A HAIR DRYER CAN HELP SPEED DRYING...

LATEX

7A.

7B.

DIP THE HAIR IN WARM WATER. WHEN IT STRAIGHTENS, LAY IT OUT IN SMALL BATCHES TO DRY...

TRIM THE BEARD ON THE ACTOR'S FACE...

MAKE SURE THE HAIR IS POINTED IN THE DIRECTION OF NATURAL GROWTH!

APPLY THE HAIR TO THE LAST "WET" LAYER...

7C.

GENTLY PRESSING WITH YOUR HANDS CAN "SHAPE" THE BEARD...

7D.

WOUNDS, BRUISES, AND "OUCHIES"

No, no, no, we must not upend the bottle of stage blood and drench ourselves! It's just not pretty! There are a few tricks to making stage wounds *effective*, instead of downright revolting! I'm always slightly amused by the gleam in people's eyes when we get to this subject. "We want realism," they cry, but the effects they are really looking for are usually found on *Science Fiction Theatre*.

Part of the "theatre magic" is being fooled into thinking you see things you don't. Allow your audience the privilege of using their dusty imaginations. If the context of your play is important and you want it to be remembered, keep the gross moments to a minimum. Otherwise the audience remembers the effects, but not the play. In brief, a little blood goes a long way!

When you begin to design for your special moment, look to your script to determine the following:

1. Does the actor have this "affliction" for the entire play? If yes, will your makeup design be a distraction to the audience? If the character does not have the affliction for the entire performance, how fast does the makeup need to be applied or removed? Do you have that much time?

2. Can the actor work inside the specially designed makeup you have in mind? It does no good to have a great makeup job that limits the actor's breathing, only to find he or she has to tap dance in it! Be a little easier on your actors.

3. Is it visual enough? It is self-defeating to have a wonderful makeup job that can't be seen by the audience because they're too far away. The highly detailed makeups on television and in the movies are not practical for the stage.

4. How safe is it for the actors? Don't run the risk of spending your opening night in the emergency room because the "really neat" stab wound actually brought out *real* blood, or because you figured the latex additions to your *eyes* were a great idea! Take safety into account at all times; no one's insurance is *that* good.

OK, now that you're properly lectured, let's try a few neat tricks.

Let's start with **a bruise.** A bruise goes through a few changes as it heals. To start off with, there is a swelling and redness. In a day you get that nice plum color. Three days will give into that purple, green, and yellow combination. In six days you'll get a green and yellow fade-out. I think the most effective bruise from stage is probably the purple and green combination. It says "ouch" very quickly to the viewer. It all depends on how long the actor is onstage, and how the play relates to the incident. You can do bruises with cream colors very well and rather quickly. They actually make a small "bruise kit," a container that has yellow, purple, green, and brown or red. Other colors you may find in bruises (and bruise kits) may be a gray or blue gray. Don't forget to powder a little. (See illustration 8a.)

How about a broken nose, or a swelling? Use either some nose putty or a lump of Derma Wax. Experiment with both—nose putty is sturdier and can handle a little more heat, but Derma Wax can be quicker to work with and remove. If your character has a misshapen nose or a lump from the start, it'll be easier. If the play has the character getting a broken nose, it's a little tricker. If you can add the "lump" at the beginning of the performance, be sure to start with a clean face, then add makeup over it. If it needs to stay on for the whole performance, use nose putty. Take a piece of nose putty and begin to roll it into a ball in your hands to make it warm and malleable. Apply some spirit gum to the skin where you want to adhere your lump. While you allow the spirit gum to get a little tacky, quickly shape the lump into the basic shape you want. Stick it onto the spirit gum and allow it to adhere for a few minutes. Then start smoothing the edges into the skin. Use a little Fixative A over the lump. This helps give some rigidity to the surface of the lump. Now do makeup as usual, being careful to not dislodge the nose putty. (See illustration 8b.)

If you need to add lumps during the performance, use a damp makeup sponge or a cotton ball with alcohol on it to remove the makeup *just in the area where you need to add the nose putty.* Blot the skin dry, add a little spirit gum, and proceed as before. Be sure to practice this even before dress rehearsals; it's very embarrassing to have your lumps melt or your nose fall off onstage.

Another way to build a **lump, false nose piece, or scar** is to use liquid latex and "theatrical tissue," or use shredded cotton balls. The best latex pieces are "vulcanized" or baked. You can buy them at a theatrical supply store. They contain no tissue or fibers (those would burn in an oven). Vul-

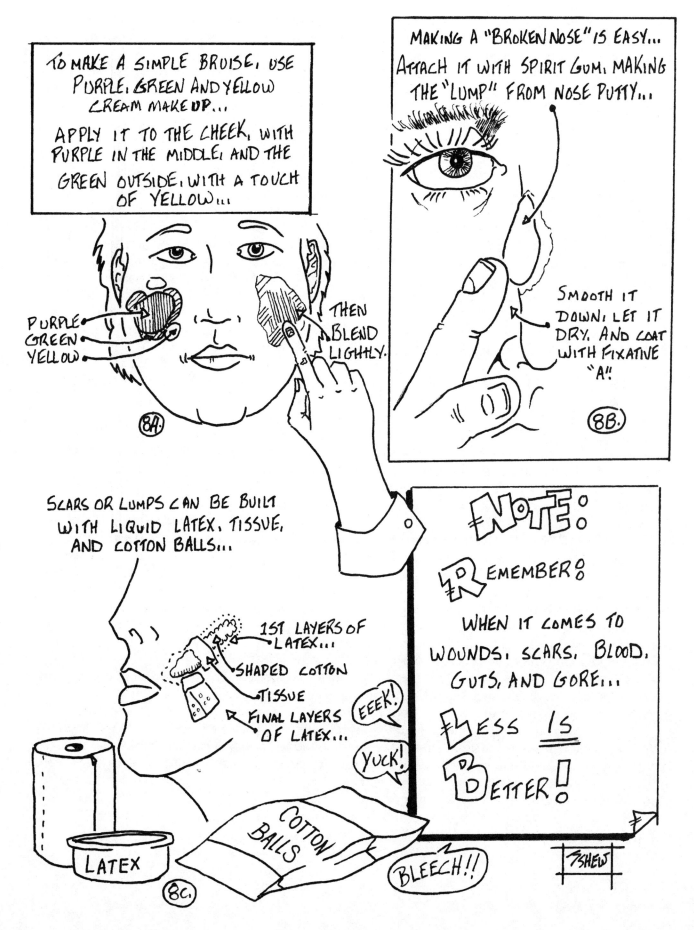

canized pieces are usually made from special molds, which you can do yourself, but it's way out of beginner territory (catch me later). The piece I'll tell you how to make is reusable but not very long-lived, maybe six performances.

Remember that liquid latex is an ammonia-based rubber product. *Be very careful around eyes, nose, and mouth.* **It will make your eyes water just using it, but it will burn mucous membranes and is toxic if swallowed!** As always, start with a clean face, splash with cool water, and pat dry. Have your materials ready before you start: disposable makeup sponge, pieces of toilet (theatrical) tissue or torn cotton balls, and a small amount of liquid latex (half an ounce to one ounce). Put your latex into a small bowl that will allow you easy access and to dip pieces of tissue. If you have a large container of liquid latex, pour a usable amount into a smaller container. This helps keep the larger portion clean and free of fibers, but also keeps it from drying out. A hair dryer is handy, too, when you *want* it to dry.

Spread a layer of liquid latex on the area that will become the surface of your added piece. Allow it to dry and become clear, add a second layer and let it dry. (See illustration 8c.) Now start with a small ball of tissue or cotton, dip it into the latex and stick it to the area on the face where you have the dried layer of latex. Add smaller balls of tissue around the base to start smoothing it out. *Keep your added pieces on the original surface area.* By now you have a nice lump, but it's not very smooth. To create a "skin" over the lump and hold it all together, take a *dry* piece of tissue and lay it over the lump. Allow the latex to absorb into it, add a little latex over the top with a sponge or your finger, and begin to smooth out the edges. As a "skin layer," you can also use a piece of nylon hosiery. (See illustration 8d.) Allow your lump to dry for 30 to 45 minutes before removing. A hair dryer can speed this up a little. To remove the piece, use a cotton ball soaked in alcohol and let it seep in around the edge, peel the piece off slowly. Allow your piece to dry for *at least 5 hours* before trying to reattach. If possible, let it dry overnight. Finish the piece with a layer of sealer, either rubber mask sealer or Fixative A. This will make the surface ready to take makeup.

Reattach the piece to your face using medical adhesive or spirit gum, *before makeup.* Do your makeup right over the top, but be careful with the piece—it's not made of steel! Use a cream base or rubber mask makeup for a large addition. Don't forget to powder.

Blood! There are two different types of stage blood, liquid and congealed. Both will give most viewers the heebie-jeebies. The liquid blood is very runny, so be careful with costumes! It will usually wash out, but don't be careless. Liquid blood is good for a quick effect. Dip a cotton swab, or use an eyedropper, and trail a little from the corner of the mouth or nose—oooh! If you need it to last a little longer, pour a little out in a container and let it start to harden up (about 20 minutes). Then apply and allow to harden and dry. It will dry in the same way syrup does, thick and sticky. It's main ingredient is corn syrup, *but don't eat it!* In addition to the coloring, it probably contains glycerine.

Liquid "blood caps" are designed for use in the mouth and are commonly used in fight scenes. The blood is released by biting down and breaking the cap. **Do not use these in your nose.** To create the "bloody nose" look while onstage, crush a blood cap in your hand as you raise it to your nose, get the blood on the end of your nose and upper lip.

My favorite blood product is the thick blood. It has a congealed consistency that really stays in place well and looks disgusting. The color indicates a deep wound, or dried blood. It is very good for quick application. You can put it on with your fingers, or a tool such as a plastic knife or spoon.

Scars can be created with tissue and latex or rigid collodion. This is a clear liquid that is actually a type of glue. It shrinks as it dries. If applied to the skin and left to dry, it puckers the skin as it dries, leaving a nice scar line. Makeup is then added on top. Again, **do not use around the eyes.** Rigid collodion should come with a brush in the bottle; if not, use a cotton swab or a disposable brush. As rigid collodion is a glue, it will render any good brush useless.

CHAPTER 5

MAKING UP CHILDREN

This can be a very fun time for everyone. It can also be very hectic and will definitely be messy. (Oops, I just described the adults' makeup room too.) The biggest difference here is that kids shouldn't be left to their own devices with makeup. Please help! Older kids (10 and up) can be taught to do their own faces at least for straight makeup, which can provide a great sense of accomplishment and responsibility! I like pulling in a few teenagers to help too. *The younger the child, the more simple the makeup should be.* They will scratch their faces, pick their noses, and rub their eyes. Don't expect them to have the discipline or patience of adults, and please don't kill the fun for them!

To start with, you must be aware that a child's skin is much more delicate and sensitive than an adult's. In both the application and removal of makeup, be very gentle. Even if you get them to wash their own faces, encourage them to be gentle on themselves and do a thorough inspection to be sure they get it all off. Children can develop reactions to irritants very quickly. **Do not use greasepaint.** Stick to cream or pancake. I don't even encourage the use of an "after-wash" treatment (such as astringent or lotion); the less you do the better.

On very small kids I suggest just getting a base on. If this is a real problem, don't force it. Let them go without makeup. My reasoning for this is: If they are too small to sit still for makeup, they probably won't be onstage long enough to worry about it. Why make the performance unpleasant for them? **This is not an argument I allow any adult to use,** although it's been tried. If the child is older or really taking to the whole experience of theatre, go ahead and finish doing a regular makeup job. Don't worry if the child can't keep it on as long.

One exception I might suggest is *not lining the eyes;* maybe use a little shadow to help define them instead. Even the most tolerant kids will blink, water, and rub their eyes when you try to put eyeliner on them.

If the performance will allow it, use a **face-painting** approach: Skip the base and just "paint" some happy designs on. Use makeup, not artist's paints, which often contain toxic chemicals. Also look into "noses" for animal faces. You can find them in most toy stores or costume shops. Just be sure that they don't block the child's nostrils, and that the "nose" has large enough holes to breathe through.

CREATING A MAKEUP NOTEBOOK

What is a makeup notebook? It's your very own, personalized resource book. **This is the place to keep notes on what works and what doesn't work for you.** It should include pictures, sketches, phone numbers, and design sheets. Anything that helps you be creative, economical, and safe when doing your face.

Start by making a copy of the design sheet in this book so that you have one on reserve for copies, and put it in an empty notebook. (See illustration 9.) Next, create a sheet that describes your straight makeup and put it in the book. Refer to this so you don't have to guess at colors, brands, or quantity when you go to restock your kit. By now you probably have started a list of what base you prefer, your best colors, facial cleansers, lotions, any allergic reactions, hair treatments, etc. I'd make sure this is easy to find in your book. Also make it easy enough to add on to as you make new discoveries. Try keeping a current list of phone numbers and addresses where you buy different makeup items. If you're in a hurry, its nice to call ahead and have it waiting. Also keep current informa-

MAKEUP DESIGN SHEET

SHOW _____

CHARACTER _____

ACTOR _____

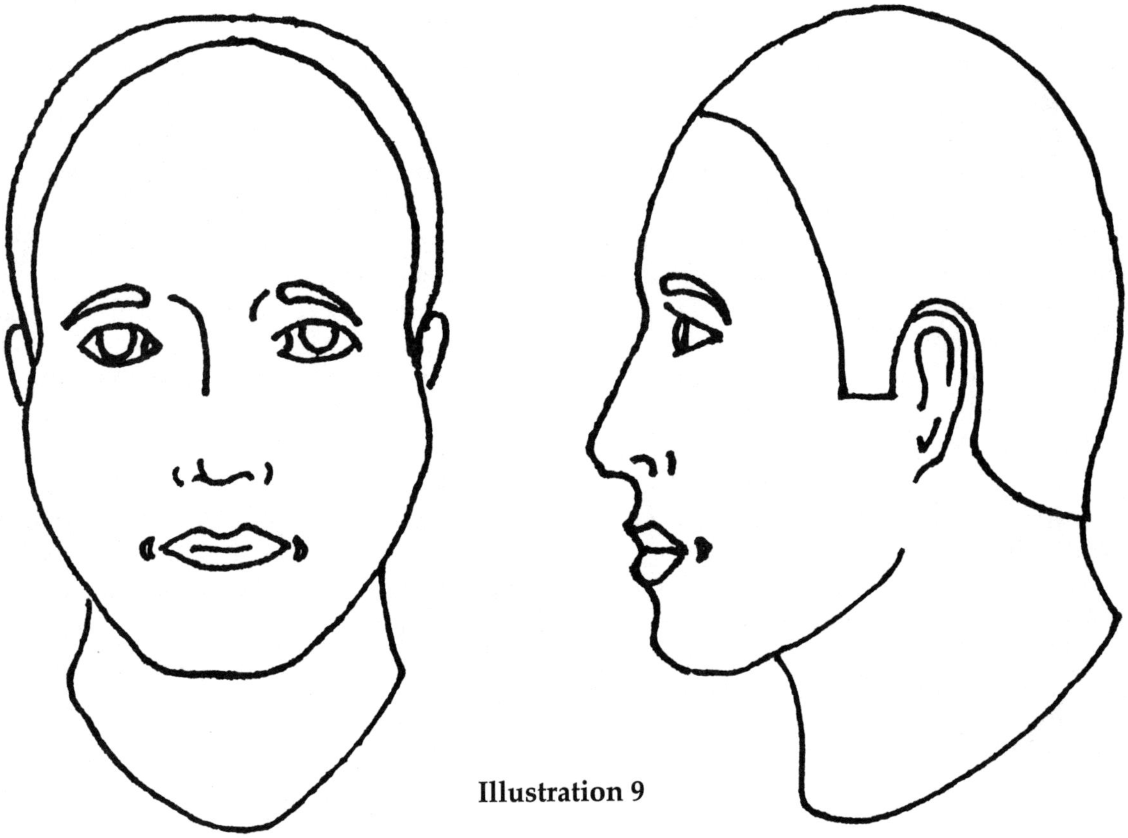

Illustration 9

BASE _____   EYE SHADOW _____

PENCIL/LINER _____   HIGHLIGHT _____

ROUGE _____   LIP COLOR _____

HAIR _____

NOTES

_____

_____

_____

(BY PERMISSION OF THE AUTHOR, THIS PAGE MAY BE PHOTOCOPIED FOR NONPROFIT USE.)

tion on the major makeup companies; they usually have a toll-free number for ordering large quantities and for answering customer questions. (See the listing at the end of this book.)

Next, start adding your design sheets that have different characters for your face. This might include middle age, old age, illness, different time periods, fantasy, ethnic, animal, or anything you have designed for your face to fit a specific role. If possible, add photographs of the design, both in profile and full face. Be sure the sheet is complete with notes on what types and colors of makeup were used, what the role was, what the performance was, average time for application, special notes on hair, and any makeup needed for neck, hands, arms, feet, etc.

Now, keep a collection of faces! Categorize types of faces to make it easier. This resource area will help you design for yourself or others. Clip pictures from magazines, newspapers, coloring books, comic books, and catalogs. (Tip: Be sure that everyone is through reading these first!)

Some suggestions for categories in your book: men, women, children, babies, ethnic groups, animals, hair designs, beard and mustache, "period" looks, and fantasy. You may wish to include a section on wounds, bruises, injuries, and illnesses. These are hard to find pictures of (and then you don't want to look at them), but on occasion you'll need to create something for effect.

THE MAKEUP ROOM—ENTER WITH ATTITUDE!

Bring your attitude of confidence and enthusiasm! In the next couple of hours this room will vibrate with energy, raw nerves, and barely controlled chaos.

It's in this room where the actors start to get a sense of "show time." All their nerves are on edge; this is it! For the actor it's a place to dump the rest of the day at the door and really focus on the character and his or her place in the performance. This is the last flurry of activity before walking onstage.

If you have a dedicated space for a makeup room that is yours, count yourself lucky. If you are in a sharing position with other groups, try to secure the space for just those performing during the run of the play. It will make everyone more comfortable. It's often necessary to leave makeup out, personal items are left there, and costumes get changed on the run. The last thing you need is curious bystanders wandering in. Everyone needs to practice courtesy and security.

"Makeup call" refers to the time you show up at the theatre to do your costume and makeup. For a director or makeup designer to establish a "call," you need to know how many people are in the cast and how large your makeup space is. The larger your cast is, the more you may need to stagger your call. People may need to arrive in shifts. Also, how many principal characters, and how many specialty makeup designs need to be executed. Most theatre groups have the rule of thumb that everyone be ready to go onstage one half hour before the curtain goes up. This allows time to fix costume problems, run lines, calm down, and basically get in character. Hopefully, most of your actors will do their own face. Try to schedule the principals first. A straight makeup will usually take 10 to 15 minutes. Allow at least one half hour for specialty designs. This is where your practice comes in handy. You should have already clocked your special items in order to schedule the call properly.

A moment of theatre tradition: the character is created solely within the confines of the theatre walls. This means that all makeup and costume are applied in the makeup room, not seen by the audience until you walk onstage, and then completely removed before leaving the building. Try to keep this in mind, but do what you must to make things run smoothly.

After a performance, try to clean up a little. Make sure the lids are on, the sinks are clean, and costumes hung up. It will make for less confusion the next performance. At the end of a show, clean up a lot. Make sure to wipe down and dry makeup bases. Find lids for everything, wash out brushes and sponges in cool soapy water, throw away sponges that have been used in latex or glue. All this goes for communal or private kits. Now is a good time to do inventory. Enclosed is a sheet you may copy, or you can develop your own. (See page 38.) Inventory sheets help you in a number of ways. You will know what colors and how many of an item you have, how old the item is, and where it's stored. (If you have to store things in someone's basement, you'll need to know what's there.)

MAKING IT ALL WORK

Now that you've got a grip on some of the basics, how do you keep the ball rolling? You need to learn where and how to shop, and how to work with your actors to bring them up to speed.

I've included current addresses and phone numbers of some of the major makeup companies in the U.S. If you have no one in your local area to help you, call or write to them directly. Get to know your local theatrical supply shops, and make friends with high schools and colleges.

If it falls at your feet to purchase makeup for a large group, you need to have a good idea of who is in your cast. I suggest separating into groups, men and women. Within those groups (actually go and look at them) decide how many light, medium, and dark bases you need. Figure a container of base to about three people, or stagger your call enough so that only two at a time need to use it. Let them know what group they are in so they can all work together. I suggest about two each of eye pencils, cheek and lip color per group of three people. If your group is small and all using the same makeup area, group them by skin tone. Just be sure to get enough variety in cheek and lip colors.

Learn to teach people to do their own makeup—it's good for everyone. Encourage them to help each other too. To do this, you say, "Did you see how I did that?" When they say yes, you smile, pat 'em on the back, and say, "Good, I'm sure you can do this yourself next time!" When they do themselves, smile again, say, "Great job!" and leave it alone. If they ask for help, give suggestions, but *let them do the work.* Eventually you'll have a group of trained people with the skill to accomplish almost everything. This will leave you free for more complex tasks.

Learn, learn, learn. You really can't know too much. Rent videos, go to the library, take a class, make a few phone calls, and have a "play day" where the whole group gets into the makeup box. I confess, I've had to learn a few things as I wrote this book. Sometimes, we must relearn. With learning comes the obligatory—practice, practice, practice. Strive for excellence, there is never enough of it!

Appendix

LEADING MAKEUP MANUFACTURERS

BEN NYE COMPANY
5935 Bowcroft St.
Los Angeles, CA 90016
(213-893-1984;
fax: 213-893-2640)

MEHRON INC.
45E Route 303
Valley Cottage, NY 10989
(1-800-332-9955;
fax: 914-268-0439)

BOB KELLY
151 W. 46th St.
New York, NY 10036
(212-819-0030;
fax: 212-869-0396)

MAKEUP INVENTORY

Bases:

Type _____ Purchase date _____

Type _____ Purchase date _____

Type _____ Purchase date _____

Liners/Brow pencils:

Color _____ Purchase date _____

Color _____ Purchase date _____

Color _____ Purchase date _____

Rouges:

Color _____ Purchase date _____

Color _____ Purchase date _____

Color _____ Purchase date _____

Lip Colors:

_____   _____

_____   _____

_____   _____

Eye Shadows:

_____   _____

_____   _____

Powder:

_____   _____

Brushes, Sponges, Puffs:

_____   _____

_____   _____

Specialty Makeup:

_____   _____

_____   _____

_____   _____

_____   _____

_____   _____

MAKEUP DESIGN SHEET

SHOW _____

CHARACTER _____

ACTOR_____

BASE _____   EYE SHADOW _____

PENCIL/LINER _____   HIGHLIGHT _____

ROUGE _____   LIP COLOR _____

HAIR _____

NOTES

_____

_____

_____